★SANTA'S★ MAGIC BAG

Written by Susan Karnovsky

Illustrated by Kathleen Dunne

Copyright © MCMXCII Playmore Inc., Publishers
and Waldman Publishing Corp., New York, New York
All rights reserved
Printed in China

Zoey Zyta lived in the last house on the last street of the very last town that Santa Claus visited.

One Christmas Eve Santa Claus forgot his magic bag and left it under Zoey's Christmas tree.

At first Zoey didn't notice the old empty bag. It was lying under the tree in a heap. In fact the bag would have been thrown away if it hadn't been for her brother Zachery.

He found it after he had opened all his other gifts — which didn't take very long — because Zachery was always the first to unwrap everything. He was also the first to ask "Are there any more?"

Zachery picked up the large sack and looked inside.

"Ahhhh!" he gasped.

Zachery was surprised because Santa's bag was magic. Anyone who looked in to Santa's bag always got whatever they wanted.

Zachery pulled out a brand new fancy computer game.

"WOW!" he screamed.

"Oh my!" said his mother.

"Well. This is quite something!" said his father.

When Zoey's mother looked in the bag,
she pulled out a beautiful, expensive sweater.
"Why, Harry! You shouldn't have!"
"I didn't!" Zoey's father replied, looking in
to the bag for some answer.

He pulled out a new fishing rod.

"What do you know!" he muttered.

"It's the one you wanted from the fancy catalogue!" Zoey's mother exclaimed.

"Henrietta?" He looked at Zoey's mother. She shrugged her shoulders and shook her head.

Meanwhile, Zoey just stood there, watching. Zoey was very different from her brother Zachery. She wasn't shy. She wasn't afraid. She just liked to look at things first — until she understood as much as she could.

Zachery grabbed the bag again and peered
in. He pulled out a new pair of boxing gloves.
"All right!!" he shouted.

He looked in again and pulled out a fancy toy truck.

"Yesss!"

Then he pulled out four new plastic action figures.
"YEAH!"

He didn't stop. He pulled out toy after toy after toy. Soon the room was filled with things he had grabbed from Santa's bag.

"The bag is magic!" he shouted.

"It's not ours," Zoey said.

"Who says? It's under our tree," Zachery shouted.

"Santa left it here and you know it."

"Finders keepers losers weepers," Zachery sneered.

"Give it to me," Zoey said.

"What are you going to go for?" Zachery asked. "Are you going to ask for a real electric car or some ponies or something neat like that?"

Zoey took the bag.

"I'm going to ask for Christmas," she whispered.

Zoey took a deep breath and looked down into the bag.

A wonderful, happy feeling filled Zoey. She laughed out loud.

Then, in the blink of an eye, the bag disappeared.
Only a small piece of gold paper remained,
fluttering to the floor.

"The bag's gone!" Zachery screamed. "You stupid! We had the bag. We could have had anything we wanted! What did you do? What did you ask for?"

"I asked for Christmas," Zoey smiled.
She was filled with a new happiness that wouldn't go away.

"That's all. I just want there to always be a Christmas — for everyone, " she said, picking up the little piece of gold paper that had fluttered to the ground.

In beautiful letters, she read the words:

Thank you
Merry Christmas
Love,
Santa